for Imogen

with love, best wishes

and a word of pictures

PETER PAN IN SCARLET

OXFORD
UNIVERSITY PRESS

Great Clarendon Street, Oxford OX2 6DP

Oxford University Press is a department of the University of Oxford.
It furthers the University's objective of excellence in research, scholarship,
and education by publishing worldwide in

Oxford   New York

Auckland   Cape Town   Dar es Salaam   Hong Kong   Karachi
Kuala Lumpur   Madrid   Melbourne   Mexico City   Nairobi
New Delhi   Shanghai   Taipei   Toronto

With offices in

Argentina   Austria   Brazil   Chile   Czech Republic   France   Greece
Guatemala   Hungary   Italy   Japan   Poland   Portugal   Singapore
South Korea   Switzerland   Thailand   Turkey   Ukraine   Vietnam

Oxford is a registered trade mark of Oxford University Press
in the UK and in certain other countries

British Library Cataloguing in Publication Data

Data available

ISBN: 978-0-19-272835-7

1 3 5 7 9 10 8 6 4 2

Printed in China

Paper used in the production of this book is a natural,
recyclable product made from wood grown in sustainable forests.
The manufacturing process conforms to the environmental
regulations of the country of origin.

Written and Adapted by

GERALDINE McCAUGHREAN

PETER PAN IN SCARLET

Illustrated by David Wyatt

OXFORD
UNIVERSITY PRESS

*T*wenty years came and went like pirate ships, and stole away their young-ness. But still the adventurers liked to lie in bed and think about Neverland. Though they were all grown up, with children of their own, Wendy and John, Slightly and Curly, and the Twins remembered their wonderful adventures with Peter Pan.

Then the dreams began.

'Last night I dreamed he flew in again at the window,' said Mr John.

'I dreamed that I could still fly,' said Doctor Curly.

'I dreamed we were back in the Neverwood,' said First Twin.

'Tinker Bell was there,' said his twin brother.

'I dreamed of the Lagoon,' said Mr Slightly.

'I was fighting Captain Hook and Starkey and Smee and the whole pirate crew!' said John, and everyone shuddered.

'I dreamed of Peter,' said Mrs Wendy. 'It was lovely.'

'Just a dream,' said Judge Tootles with a shrug.

But that was not quite true.

Dreams don't usually leave leftovers in your bed. These ones did: swords, clocks, hats . . . and even a hook!

'Something is wrong,' said Wendy. 'Dreams are leaking out of Neverland. That is why we must go back.'

'Go back? Nonsense!' protested the others. 'How? Grown-ups can't go to Neverland!'

'Then we must grow young again,' said Wendy quietly.

'But we can't fly any more!' said Tootles. 'Not without fairy dust!'

'Then we must find some fairy dust,' said Wendy simply.

'But we don't know any fairies!' said Slightly.

'So find one, gentlemen,' said Wendy, collecting up the teacups. 'Remember what Peter Pan told us? When a

baby laughs for the first time, a fairy is born. Find me a baby, gentlemen, and make it laugh!'

Well, finding a baby was easy, but making it laugh?

They tried everything—jokes, tickling, pulling faces, and blowing raspberries—until . . .

. . . Slightly started singing . . .

That baby's laugh hatched like an egg. And there he was at last.

'I'm Fireflyer and I'm HUNGRY!'

So they took him to the tea rooms and fed him on cake crumbs and cool tea, then carried him home in John's hat. His little body fizzed, hot as a light bulb. By the time they got home, the hat was quite scorched, but it was half full of fairy dust.

Fireflyer was always hungry and he told awful lies. Fairies do, you know: they are even proud of it.

'Do you know Tinker Bell?' asked Mr John.

'Of course. I know everything,' said Fireflyer. 'What's a Tinker Bell?'

The Twins explained how once they had lived in Neverland with Peter Pan and his trusty helper Tinker Bell the Fairy.

'She was rather bad-tempered, but very beautiful,' they said, remembering.

'Not as beautiful as me!' said Fireflyer and ate another candle. 'All the world over I'm famously beautiful and clever!'

When Slightly called him 'the most terrific fibber', Fireflyer was so pleased that, from then on, he loved Slightly better than anything.

(Except eating, of course.)

*T*ime to leave for Neverland!

Sure enough, Fireflyer knew a way for them to grow young again. (I expect you found out years ago.) So one night, when the moon was as round and shiny as pirate silver, they stole their own children's clothes and put them on. (Well, everyone knows: when you put on dressing-up clothes, you turn into someone else.)

Come bathtime, the Twins stole school uniforms from their twin sons.

Dr Curly stole a sports shirt and shorts after his boy had fallen asleep.

Mr John told stories of Neverland to his own little boy . . . then, as soon as the child was dreaming, stole a sailor suit.

10

'Goodness me!' said Tootles with a gulp. 'I quite forgot: my child's a girl!'

Mrs Wendy wrote a note saying that she was going to visit a distant friend. Then she put on her daughter Jane's sundress and kissed the sleeping girl goodbye. At the last moment, a big sneeze made her snatch up her handkerchief and tuck it into the sleeve of the sundress.

But as the others got ready to go, Slightly sat alone at home, playing unhappy tunes on his clarinet.

'So I won't be going, after all,' he whispered sadly to himself. Slightly had no children, you see.

As they combed fairy dust into their hair, the adventurers forgot all kinds of grown-up things. But they did not forget their children, of course. Mothers and fathers could never do that.

11

*I*n the sky over London, a flock of children swam and
swooped and whooped with joy, perching like
birds on the tops of buildings.

Curly had brought his son's puppy along by accident.

'Tootles? Is that really you?' asked John.

'Yeth, and aren't I pretty?' said the girl in the ballet
dress, and twirled on tiptoe.

But there was no sign of Slightly, or his clarinet. That
was when Wendy remembered: 'The poor darling has
no children to change clothes with! He won't be able
to come!'

'Oh yes I will!'

And there he was, plunging through the air like a porpoise. 'I went down to the end of the bed!' he called. 'I remembered, you see? All kinds of magic can happen if you go right down to the end!'

Fireflyer didn't know the way to Neverland, of course, because he had only just been born. Luckily everyone else remembered:

'Second to the right and straight on till morning!'

'Out of my way, clouds!'
cried John. 'I can't wait to
see Neverland again.'

'Will Tinker Bell be there?'
demanded Fireflyer impatiently.
'Tell me!'

'Are we nearly there yet?'
said the Twins, as night
turned to morning.

The clouds parted, and there it lay below them: Neverland, totally and absolutely and utterly . . . CHANGED.

Summer had turned to autumn. The sea was stormy and black. Shadows were long, the wind was bitter.

The Wendy House now perched high in the branches of the Nevertree. Cold and weary, the travellers landed on its roof and clung to it, knocking and calling . . . 'Peter! Peter Pan!' But nobody came. So Wendy pushed open the door.

There stood Peter Pan, sword drawn. His leafy clothes —once summer green—were the colour of autumn now, and he scowled with rage.

'Have at you, Nightmares!'

Wendy put her hands on her hips. 'Is that any way to greet your old friends, Peter?'

'I have no friends who are old!' cried the boy with the sword.

Wendy's eyes filled with tears, to think that Peter could have forgotten them.

'Don't be silly,' she said crossly. 'I am Wendy and we have come . . . we have come . . .'

Unfortunately, now that Wendy was a girl again, she could not quite remember why she and the boys had come.

Peter looked at her more closely. 'Oh. Is it you?' he said uncertainly. 'I thought I was dreaming you. I dreamed you a lot lately. You were much too big.' (Dreams had been leaking into Neverland as well, you see.) 'But now you're here, we can have the best adventures!' And he put back his head and crowed for joy: **'Cock-a-doodle-doo!'**

'First of all you must promise not to do any growing-up,' said Peter. And they did. 'Tomorrow we'll go and do something terrifically brave . . . but today we'll play Pretend.'

And they did.

They clean forgot about bad dreams and how everything was darkly different in Neverland. Peter did not seem to have noticed that anything was wrong.

Fireflyer kept asking about Tinker Bell the Famous Fairy—'Is she here?' 'Is she hiding?' 'Is she dead?' 'Does she know about me?'

But Peter must have forgotten all about Tinker Bell, too.

They ate a delicious dinner of pretend food, and warmed themselves in front of a blazing, imaginary fire. (Peter can pretend things better than anyone.)

Oh, and nobody thinks up such good games, either. Wendy and John, Slightly, Curly, and the Twins quickly forgot why they had come. They were having such fun they did not care that the weather outside was windy wild, that thunder thumped and rain ripped leaves off the trees.

But in the night, when they were all asleep, a lick of lightning lashed the Nevertree and—CRACK!—the Wendy House toppled and fell—over and over and D
O
W
N.

They landed on mountains of crisp leaves, down in the deep, damp dark of the Neverwood.

'Is everyone all right?' asked Wendy and lent Peter her handkerchief, because he had banged his nose. 'Don't worry. Tomorrow we will all help to build a new house.'

'Oh no we won't,' said Peter cheerfully. 'We'll go exploring!'

And that's what they did, though mud sucked at their shoes and the rain ran down their necks.

'Whatever happened to summer?' asked Curly, shivering, but Peter was not missing the fine weather. He loved the place, cold or warm, wet or dry.

Exploring brought them to the shore of the lagoon, where the sea surf slopped in big oily waves over the bones of mermaids. And that was where Tootles found it. In fact she sat right down on top of it.

'Dragondragondragondragondragondragoooon!' said Princess Tootles, as the jaws swung open.

'That's not a dragon,' snorted John.

'No. It's a nalligator,' said First Twin.

'Dragon,' said Tootles, sulking.

'It's very dead, whatever it is,' said Curly, holding his nose.

'It's a nalligator,' said Second Twin.

'It's not neither, so there!' said Tootles. 'Anyone can see it's a . . .'

'Crocodile,' said Wendy calmly. 'It is a crocodile. In fact it is the very crocodile who swallowed our old enemy Captain Hook. There's the alarm clock that ticked in its stomach all those years, remember? Hook was scared silly when he heard that tick-tock-tick.'

Could it really be twenty years since Peter Pan had fought the villainous pirate Captain Hook and sent him overboard into the jaws of the waiting crocodile?

'Where are we going to sleep tonight?'
whined Tootles, but no one answered.

They had just noticed the bears coming
towards them along the beach. Behind
them came a man with a whip.

'Please do not let my cubs frighten you,'
said the man.

'Nothing frightens me!' boasted Peter Pan.

The Great Ravello smiled and bowed very
low. 'Of course not. You are the marvellous
Peter Pan, the One-and-Only, the Boy-who-
Never-Grows-Up. I have longed to meet
you. But is it not rather late and
chilly for young people to
be out? Let me offer you
a bed for the night.
Follow me to Circus
Ravello: some of my
animal cages are
empty and the straw is
soft and dry.'

Peter scowled. 'We don't go
about with grown-up people

—nor we don't sleep in cages.'

'But you will come to see the show, at least!' said the Great Ravello. 'My lions and acrobats and clowns? Everyone loves the circus.'

'Oh yes, Peter, a circus!' cried the others.

But Peter scowled. 'I don't like clowns. You can't tell what they're thinking.'

Sadly the Great Ravello bowed again and turned away. His bears went dancing after him into the fog.

Cold and tired now, the explorers began to complain and quarrel. 'That ravelling man might have given us eggy and toast,' said Fireflyer, and Peter knocked him into a rock pool.

' "Travelling man", not "ravelling man",' said Wendy and pulled him out again.

Then Peter sniffed the air. 'Is that smoke?' he said.

he Neverwood was burning. It glowed orange. The fire roared like a thousand bears, and into the sky rose a circus tent, ablaze.

The children had nowhere to run. Behind them, the burning forest; in front of them, the heaving sea. John's eyes grew wide.

'Sail ho!'

Looming out of the smoky darkness came a ship. It ran aground on the beach.

'It is his ship!' breathed Peter. 'Hook's ship.'

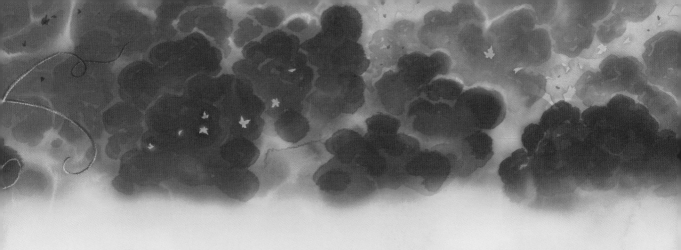

The little ones were afraid to go aboard, but Peter led the way. 'What are you scared of? Hook's long gone. That crocodile swallowed him!'

Wendy climbed up too, sparks swirling round her head. Flames were flapping. The smoke was choking thick. 'Come along, little ones,' she called. 'Follow me.'

In the nick of time, the *Jolly Roger* floated out to sea and carried them safely out of the burning bay. They tugged down the pirate flag and Wendy made a new one from her sundress. As she said, 'We are not pirates, are we?'

For twenty years, Captain Hook's ship had floated empty over the sea. For twenty years, no one had walked its decks. No one had opened the door of the captain's cabin. No one had opened the sea chest inside. That was where Peter found the telescope—

'Curly, you can be look-out.'

—the ship's compass—

'John, you can navigate.'

—the white shirt and even whiter tie—

'Stand still while I tie it for you, Peter.'

—and the scarlet coat.

'Hook's second-best coat,' said Peter, putting it on. 'He was wearing his best one when the crocodile got him.'

Then he climbed the mast and crowed so loudly that the stars blinked. 'Rename the ship *Jolly Peter*, and I shall be Captain Pan and sail the seven seas!'

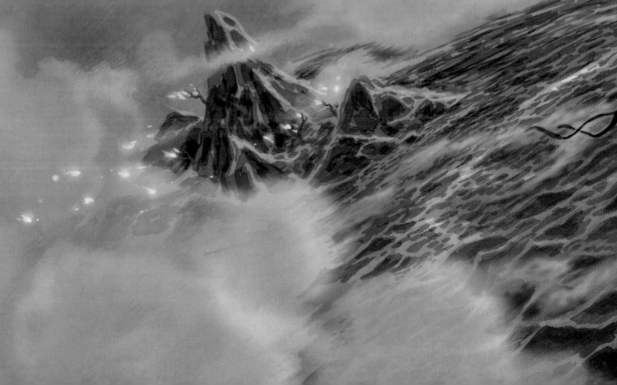

Sinking his hands in the pocket of the
red coat, he felt something there,
papery and crumpled.

'A treasure map! And here's where Hook
stowed his treasure. Put on sail, you lubbers!
We're going on a treasure hunt!'

Up in his crow's-nest, Curly looked through his telescope and saw islands and whales, lighthouses and albatrosses; saw sunsets and seagulls and shipwrecks.

One day, though, he saw . . . 'Pirates!'

The steamship rammed the *Jolly Peter*. Over the rails came dozens of small pirates, with bows, arrows, hatchets, and knives between their teeth. They tied up John, Wendy, and the rest, but dared not go near Peter,

fierce and fearless, with his dagger in his hand.

'Turn out your pockets, matey,' called the pirate captain, 'and hand over everything. Cos it's mine now.'

Peter thought about the treasure map in his pocket. Let it fall into pirate hands? 'Never!' he cried.

'Then shoot him full of arrows, my buckos!' and the little pirates drew back their bowstrings and took aim on Peter's heart.

Just then, a little island sailed by, towing behind it a chain of smaller islands. One had a cargo of bears, one of monkeys. One carried horses with feathers in their brow bands. The island in front carried the single, shaggy shape of a man.

'May I be of help, your lordship?' called the Great Ravello and cracked his circus whip.

First aboard the ship were the bears, their furry fatness flopping on to the deck.

The little pirates ran and shut themselves in the hold.

The big bears dipped their huge paws in through the hatches, claws as sharp as dinner knives. The pirate captain tried to sneak away, but Ravello brought him back.

'Hand over your cargo!' Peter called after him. 'Cos it's mine now.'

'Take it!' whimpered the captain. 'If you want a ton of onions! Take it all!'

But greedy little Fireflyer had already squeezed into the hold of the pirate ship and eaten every bit.

'Hic!'

'Lock that fairy up below decks!' raged Pan. 'The little thief has eaten our booty!'

And suddenly the boy in the red coat was very scary indeed. Even Wendy and the boys trembled to see the way he shouted and stamped about the deck.

Almost like a pirate.

Again Ravello bowed low to Peter Pan. 'My circus life is over, my tent burned. A sad day indeed . . . But let me travel with you, and oh, what joy! I long to serve the magnificent, the marvellous Peter Pan! Let me be your servant!—your valet!—butler to the Wonderful Boy!'

Peter liked the sound of 'magnificent' and 'marvellous' and 'wonderful'. He also liked the way Ravello cooked him breakfast, cleaned his boots, and brushed down his scarlet coat.

Of course, Peter took off the red coat when he went swimming.

He swam down to steal swords from the swordfish, so that the League of Pan would have proper weapons at their waists.

Then they all crossed swords and swore again never to grow up, and Peter swore to lay down his life for his friends (if he had to). Then Ravello hurried his arms back into the sleeves of the scarlet coat, '. . . before you catch your death of cold, m'lord.'

In fact Ravello made himself wonderfully useful. In his long life he had travelled to every corner of Neverland, and knew it better even than Peter.

When the ship began to slip fast and faster through the waves, it was Ravello who guessed why. 'Lodestone Reef! Its magnetism is pulling her in!'

'Don't be silly: the ship is wooden,' John snorted.

'But her nails are iron,' said Ravello. 'Save yourselves!'

Lodestone Rock sucked every nail out of the wooden ship. The *Jolly Peter* fell to pieces around them. The bears were first to leap overboard.

'Fly!' cried Peter and everyone leapt into the air.

Except for Ravello, of course.

He rowed ashore astride the sea chest, calling:

'Behold Grief Reef, m'lord. Once upon a time all the wrecks you see here were prams. Prams wheeled in parks by nursemaids. Prams with babies in them. Prams without babies in them. Boys fell out of them and were lost. And you well know what happens to Lost Boys.'

Tootles knew. 'They are posted to Neverland to live with Peter Pan, of course.'

'And what becomes of the nursemaids who lost them?' The children shook their heads, so Ravello explained. 'They are so furious that they set sail in their empty prams and come here to hunt down the wretched babies who got themselves lost.'

The Twins shut their eyes tight with fright:

'But they can't get into Neverland, can they? . . . because they are grown-ups and grown-ups can't!'

Ravello took a rubbery egg from his pocket and ate it thoughtfully. 'Quite right. They can get only as far as the Maze over there. And that makes them so raging mad that—pfff!—they turn into witches.'

'Behold the Maze of Witches,' said Ravello. 'Whatever you do, don't let them catch you, or they will wash you and iron you and eat you like toast.'

Soft-footed, the explorers tried to creep through the Maze of Witches. But it had so many twists and turns! Soon they were all as lost as Yesterday.

Through its twisting lanes, a hundred women crawled and called and searched. Round the next corner, the explorers came face-to-face with one of the witches.

She gave such a shriek that other women came running, hands reaching and snatching . . . 'Children! There are children!'

Soon they were completely surrounded by wild-haired wailing women. It seemed impossible that the explorers would ever get away from all those clutching hands.

So Slightly put his clarinet to his lips and played.

The women stopped. The women even listened. They sighed, sobbed, and swayed—couldn't help it: the sad, lilting music held them spellbound.

Wendy, Tootles, John, the Twins, and even Peter picked up their feet and ran. Behind them came Ravello, pulling the sea chest behind him.

But Slightly played on and on. Soon the witches' eyes were too full of tears to see.

That was when Slightly seized his chance and ran.

'Oh, Slightly, you were wonderful!' his friends greeted him.

'Three cheers for Slightly!'

'Slightly saved us!'

Slightly blushed with pleasure, but he was uneasy in his mind about the weeping women.

'Those ladies . . . are you sure they are witches?' he asked the circus master.

Ravello did not answer: he was too busy clapping. 'Such talent, Master Slightly! Surely this is what you want to be in life! A musician? When you grow up?'

Slightly imagined it for a moment: he a grown man in an evening suit, standing on a stage, making music for a host of happy faces.

'Oh yes!' he sighed. 'I'd love that!' And Ravello's eyes flashed with joy.

'Then nothing can stop you, boy. Nothing can stop you.'

*T*hey walked on through thorns and nettles, over moors and hills. Each mealtime Ravello opened the sea chest, took out a cloth and spread it on the ground, and Peter imagined them a meal—whatever they wanted. They all agreed. 'Peter does the most delicious imagining.' And while they ate, Ravello combed Peter's hair until it was glossy, dark, and curled right down to his shoulders. Whenever Peter took off his scarlet coat, Ravello begged him to put it on again. '. . . You have a nasty cough, m'lord. You really must keep warm.'

The Great Ravello, though, never sat down to eat with them. His many pockets seemed to be full of rubbery, grey eggs, and these he ate for breakfast, lunch, and dinner. He did not sleep, either, but sat up all night long, keeping guard over the sleeping adventurers.

Neverland was full of wonders. Rivers flowed uphill. Flowers opened their petals and sang. Trees snatched birds out of the sky and ate them. Stones floated. But most wonderful of all was the waterfall where they stopped to drink. Its spray was rainbowy in the sunshine. Even the sky seemed to be suddenly full of rainbows.

In fact, the sky was raining colour.

'Fairies!' cried Tootles in delight. 'Thousands of fairies.'

At first it was pretty.

Then it was odd.

Then it was scary.

Then it was heavy—heavy as a haystack.

'What side? What side? What side are you?
Are you Red or are you Blue?
Answer now and answer true:
Are you Red or are you Blue?'

The Fairies of Neverland were at war with each other, because they could not agree which colour was best: red or blue.

'Are you Blue or are you Red?
Take a side or you are dead.'

The children did not want to choose. 'We are not on any side!' gasped Wendy. 'We are explorers!'
But the fairies would not listen.

'Show your banner, Blue or Red.
Show your flag or lose your head.
Nothing else will rescue you.
Are you Red or are you Blue?'

Peter tried to tell them, too: 'How can we raise our flag unless you get off us!'
But the fairies were not listening.

'Say what colour flag you fly.
If you don't, prepare to die.
One... two...'

'Rainbow!' Peter wriggled out from under the mountain of fairies. He snatched the rainbow out of the waterfall and waved it like a banner. 'Rainbow. That's our flag!'

The fairies squealed in wonder. They could see blue and red . . . and every other colour. Confused, they let go and fell (fairies always fall upwards, you know) and the explorers were free.

But they were sad to think of the fairies fighting. 'They never used to fight,' said Curly.

'It never used to rain,' said the Twins.

'I'm hungry,' said Fireflyer (as usual).

They came to a tree full of delicious berries. Peter flew up into the branches. He looked so fine up there in his scarlet jacket and shiny boots, laughing to see the others jumping and stretching, not able to reach. All their fairy dust had washed off in the rain. Then Slightly came along and picked a bunch of berries and gave them to Wendy.

'Cut the name out of that boy and never speak it again!' shouted Peter. 'Slightly has grown!'

In his rage, he drew his sword and cut a door in the air. Driving Slightly out, he slammed the door shut. 'Slightly is banished to Nowhereland for breaking his promise and growing bigger.'

They had never seen Peter so angry. He was like a different person.

*T*he next time Ravello spread the cloth for dinner, Peter shut his eyes and imagined as hard as he could. The children reached out for their imagined supper.

Nothing.

'I can't—' whispered Peter fearfully, then he gave Ravello a push and stood up. 'I can't be bothered,' he said.

Six little stomachs grumbled with hunger. Had Peter truly lost his magical imagination? No one dared to ask: he had become so bad tempered lately.

'Do not worry, little children,' said Ravello in his deep and gravelly voice. 'I saw sea-biscuits in the sea chest this morning.'

But no. Greedy little Fireflyer had eaten every one.

Peter was furious. 'Thieving fairy! I banish you to Nowhereland for stealing rations!' And he drew his sword, and cut a window in the air. Then he shooed Fireflyer through, and shut the window—bang! 'Never let me see you again!' shouted Captain Pan.

Fireflyer and Slightly met up in Nowhereland. Fireflyer had always liked Slightly best. Now Slightly played sad tunes on his clarinet, and Fireflyer ate the notes out of the air. (They tasted like chocolates.)

'We hate him, don't we?' said Fireflyer, munching.

'Probably not,' said Slightly.

'Tell me a story,' said Fireflyer.

So Slightly told him stories from the Past—about Tinker Bell the brave fairy, about crocodiles and nursemaids and warrior princesses; about Captain James Hook the wickedest pirate on all the seven seas.

'What was Hook like?' asked Fireflyer.

Slightly thought back. 'Ooo, he shouted a lot and swaggered about and bragged, and he was mean to his men.'

'Just like Peter, you mean?' said Fireflyer through a mouthful of music.

'No, no! Not one bit!' Slightly protested. But a little voice inside his heart kept telling him: Peter Pan in his coat of scarlet had begun to behave exactly like Captain James Hook.

At the top of Neverpeak lay Hook's buried treasure.
At the bottom of Neverpeak stood Peter Pan and his brave treasure-seekers, shivering with cold.

'Fly up there for us, Peter, and fetch it down,' whined Tootles.

'Lazy moll!' bawled Peter, and made Tootles cry.

They climbed up sticky, prickling trees towards a ledge of rock. Wasps stung them, twigs scratched, birds dropped stones on them. 'This is no fun any more,' they whimpered. 'Can the treasure be worth all this?'

'Of course,' said Ravello, 'or it would not be treasure.'

Remember, treasure in Neverland isn't always gold and jewels. It is whatever you wish for most. The chest on Neverpeak—if it could be found—would contain someone's dearest wish. But whose?

'I wish for books,' said Wendy.

'The key to a palace!' said Tootles.

'A silver sword for me!'

'All the sweets I can eat!'

'Something shiny,' said Peter in a puzzled voice, 'I dreamed it, but I don't know what it was.'

'And what do you wish for, Mr Ravello?'

'I cannot wish, Miss Wendy,' said the travelling, ravelling man. 'No more than I can sleep.'

It was true: Peter's servant never slept. He kept guard every night, watching for danger, eating rubbery eggs from the pockets of his shaggy cardigan.

Peter's temper had passed, too. Despite the cold wind, he was sweating. His cheeks were fiery red, and he had taken off his scarlet coat. But when he looked round and saw their faces, he smiled.

'Courage, friends. Did we think this would be easy? No! But we came this far and we can go the rest of the way! Not everyone can be rich or beautiful or clever, but we can all be brave. If we tell our hearts "Don't jump about", we can all be heroes. Courage is what matters, isn't that right, friends?'

Beautiful in his white shirt, with the wind in his hair, Peter put new heart into them. He made each one of them feel like a hero in a story.

Earlier on, they had not wanted to go one step further with the unkind, shouting boy in the scarlet coat. Now they were ready to follow him to the end of the world (or the top of Neverpeak, which is almost the same).

Up and up they climbed. When they got tired, Ravello said, 'Your shadows are weighing you down. Better let me look after them.' And he trimmed away the trailing black of their shadows.

Peter would not part with his—'No! Never!'

But before long, he was more weary than anyone, white-faced and coughing. 'Do it, then,' he snapped.

Puppy must have thought that it hurt, because he ran in and nipped Ravello, who snatched up the little dog, glaring at it.

'Is it your wish, mutt, to grow up into a big dog?' hissed the ravelling man. Then his temper passed and he set Puppy gently down again.

Lovingly, he folded Peter's shadow and tucked it inside his huge, shaggy cardigan, along with the others.

'Your coat, m'lord, or you may catch your death,' urged Ravello. 'Please, your excellency. It is snowing.'

Then they came to the ice bridge, and their small hearts quailed at the sight of it.

So slippery. So high. So narrow.

Such a long way down.

'Follow me!' cried Peter, fearless as ever, and ran out onto the beam of ice. But halfway across, his feet slipped and, with a fearful cry, he plunged over the edge.

'Hold on, boy! I'm coming!' cried Ravello, and took— one—two—three leaping strides. His boots holed the

ice bridge and down slid legs and body, as far as his shoulders. 'Grab my legs, boy! I'll pull you up!'

Fist closed tight around a single fragile icicle, Peter sobbed salt tears into the buffeting wind.

'I can't fly, Ravello. Why can't I fly?'

Slowly, painfully, his servant drew Peter back through the hole in the bridge and held him close. 'There, there, lad. Just think of the treasure waiting up there. The thought will warm you.'

Peter had already dreamed of the treasure in the treasure chest. He did not know where the dreams came from, but his head was full of the shapes of shiny, wonderful things. They had no name, but he knew that he wanted them more than anything in the world.

'Where's Puppy?' asked Curly. 'I can't find Puppy!'

'Maybe he fell off the mountain,' said John.

'Maybe he met Tinker Bell and she ate him!' suggested Fireflyer.

'Maybe he went back down to wait for us,' said Wendy, which was much more comforting.

The explorers sang as they climbed.

'To the top, we're going right to the top;
From the capital letter to the last full stop,
From the very first sip to the final drop;
That's where we're going: right to the top!

All the way we're going; we're going all the way
From the first crack of dawn to the close of the day,

No matter what the scaredy-cats and don't-believers say
That's where we're going: we're going all the way!'

They were still trying to wish the treasure chest full
of good things, but their wishes were rather different
now.

'I am wishing for fairy dust to get us safe home,' said
Wendy.

'I'm wishing for firewood to build a fire.'

'I'm wishing for food and a hot drink.'

'I wish I knew where Puppy went,' said Curly, because
this was no place for a little puppy, lost and all alone.

'All the way we're going; we're going all the way,
Right from Sunday morning up to Saturday,
Eating flying fishes on the road to Mandalay!
All the way we're going, we're going all the way!
And if you don't believe us, we're going anyway!
We're going all the way, we are! We're going all the way!'

Suddenly they could not climb any more, because
they were at the top.

What a view!
From the top of
Neverpeak, you can
see beyond Belief.

*S*now covered everything. Peter dug with his sword, dug with his hands. 'Where is it? Where? It should be here!—Yes!'

Something red showed beneath the snow. A scarlet trunk. Peter broke his swordfish sword opening the lock.

And there inside were:

'Firewood!'

'Rice pudding!'

'Fairy dust!'

'Bones?' (Puppy must have been wishing, too.)

'Tinker Bell? Oh, Peter, how lovely! You wished for Tink!'

But Peter had not wished the fairy there. Fireflyer had done that. Peter's wish lay under all the rest, filling most of the chest. Cups and trophies, medals and prizes: these were Peter's treasure. One by one he and Ravello lifted them out and sat them down in the snow.

'They are very pretty, Peter,' said Wendy, 'but what are they?'

Cold and sleepy, Tinker Bell looked up at him, too. 'That's not Peter,' she murmured. 'For a moment I thought it was. But he's the other one.'

'It's true,' said Peter, staring in terror at his own reflection in a shiny silver cup. 'It's true, Wendy. I am not me.'

Ravello gave the strangest laugh. 'Not yourself, Peter Pan? Quite right. Don't you know? When a boy puts on different clothes, he becomes someone else.'

The Twins were busy piling up firewood for a bonfire. 'Ravello, come and help us!' they begged. But Ravello ignored them.

'Not yourself? No! For you have become Captain James Hook . . . Oh, what a kindness you did me, Pan, the day you put on my second-best coat!'

HOOK?!

The ravelling, travelling man kicked Peter aside and gloried in the treasure. 'Not any more. Once I was Hook, in a scarlet coat and sea boots, my hair long and dark and curled. But not since the crocodile. Oh, it is a terrible place, the inside of a crocodile, believe me. It . . . frazzles a man. There I lay, an alarm clock sticking in my back, and I passed the time thinking of my treasure, and of Revenge.

'Do you remember how I always carried a bottle of poison on me? Well, that bottle broke and leaked: poisoned the crocodile, poisoned the lagoon, poisoned Neverland, look. By the time I cut my way out, Neverland was changed and so was I . . . into THIS. A soft, ravelled thing that cannot sleep, that cannot wish.

'So I combed the Peter out of Pan and I combed my hopes into your head . . . In short I made you do my wishing for me. And here it is: the treasure I left here all those years ago. My first pirate booty! My school sports cups.'

'You stole your school cups?!'

'Terrible, I know. Once upon a time I could have won them all, fair and square. I was the best sportsman in my school. My mother, though, was not a good sport. She took me out of school simply to save money. That is mothers for you.

'So I stole the cups and fled, by air balloon, and came here where heartless mothers can be forgotten. Crashing here on Neverpeak, I abandoned my precious treasure and dragged myself down to the lagoon and a life of wickedness . . . Now at last I have returned to find what I hid here. . . . And you have found it for me, Captain Cock-a-doodle.'

'No!' cried Peter. He pulled off the coat (though the wind was bitter cold).

'No hard feelings, boy,' said the ravelling man. 'You have the makings of a first-rate pirate.'

'Never!' cried Peter and tried to pull the white tie from round his throat.

'No? What, then? An actor? An acrobat? An explorer? Yes! That's it! An explorer. Is that what you would like to be? When you grow up? Is it? Is it?'

Peter started to say that explorers were better than pirates. He started to imagine how it would be to discover new lands and . . .

'Don't answer him, Peter!' A figure appeared through the falling snow.

It was Slightly. He had grown so tall that his evening shirt almost fitted him. 'Don't answer him, Peter! That is how he does it, you see. That is how he tricks children into growing. He asks them: what do you want to be when you grow up?'

Hook snarled. 'Curse you, Slightly. Another moment and I might have stolen childhood for ever from the Boy-Who-Never-Grows-Up.'

'Let's fly home now,' said Tootles, gibbering with cold. 'Do let's.'

Hook smiled the smile of a shark. 'What, without these, my dear?' And he pulled out their folded shadows from under his coat. 'I fear it cannot be done. No one can fly without their shadow.'

Opening his fist he let the shadows go. Their dark shapes danced away and away on the wind until they were swallowed up by a whirling whiteness.

A blizzard was blowing towards Neverpeak.

'Help us light the bonfire, Ravello, or we'll all die of cold!' called John.

72

The ravelling man took out a box of matches and shook it. One match left. 'What's the little word that gets things done?' he asked sweetly.

'PLEASE!' said everyone, except for Peter.

But Ravello only struck the last match, held it up, and let the blizzard blow it out.

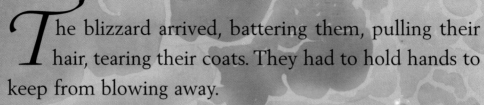

*T*he blizzard arrived, battering them, pulling their hair, tearing their coats. They had to hold hands to keep from blowing away.

But one snowflake that flew by was not like the rest. This one glowed red. This one was hot. This one was Fireflyer.

'Oh!' cried Tinker Bell when she saw him.

'Oh!' cried Fireflyer when he saw Tinker Bell, so cold, so pretty, so in danger of dying.

And do you know what he did next?

He said, 'I'm not going to light that fire. You needn't think I am!' Then he plunged into the bonfire.

Well, he always was a fearful liar—and the flicker of his fiery wings set the wood blazing.

'No, no! Fireflyer will be all burned up!' howled Tootles.

'What a fairy!' whispered Peter in horror.

'What a fairy!' exclaimed Tinker Bell in delight, and she too plunged into the bonfire.

Together, the magic of the fairies was three times as big. That bonfire burned as high as the sky. It melted the snow. It frightened off the blizzard. It unfroze the mountain from head to foot and warmed the children like a summer sun.

They made tea and drank a toast to the two brave fairies who had given their lives to save the day. But they could not be anything but sad, knowing they had lost the two bravest fairies in Neverland.

Two dirty smuts blew out of the bonfire and settled in Curly's teacup—*SPLASH*. Like a fortune-teller, Curly stared into his cup.

The smuts began to swim about. The tea turned a dirty black. 'Tink? Fireflyer? Is it really you?' whispered Curly, and the other children crowded round to look.

'Pass the soap, Tink,' said Fireflyer splashing tea everywhere.

'Silly boy,' said Tinker Bell, and threw a sugar lump at him.

After that, Tinker Bell and Fireflyer spoke only to each other and no one else, because they were so much in love. They were not interested in any treasure. They were not interested in the summery weather. For the first time, Fireflyer was not even hungry—well, not for half an hour, anyway.

'We're going down now. Come, if you are coming!' called Peter. But the fairies only jumped into the empty treasure chest and pulled shut the lid with a BANG. When Curly opened it again, there was nothing and no one inside.

Going Down should have been easy. The weather was warm. The snow was gone.

But Peter grew more and more pale, more and more weary. He pulled at the tie round his neck. He tripped and tumbled and fell, and each time he took longer to get up again.

But the other explorers were busily hurrying down Neverpeak, looking for the fairies, looking for Puppy. They would not speak one word to Hook, but he too was climbing down the mountain.

None of them noticed when Peter started to cough. He coughed and coughed until all his strength was gone. He coughed and coughed until he stumbled and fell, tumbling down the mountainside, to lie like a boy dead.

'You have killed him, Hook!'

'Not I,' protested Hook.

'Yes, your white tie choked him!'

'No!' roared Hook.

'Well then, you poisoned him, like you poisoned all Neverland!'

'I deny it!'

'Well then, you broke his heart, you beast!'

'Not I.'

'What does it matter?' sobbed Tootles. 'Peter Pan is dead.'

A quiver went through Neverland then. All the reflections climbed out of the pools and lakes, and shivered on the banks. The moon was white-faced with fright.

Tootles covered Peter with his wonderful rainbow banner and began to cry.

Hook glanced down at his sworn enemy. 'He is certainly dying, but he is not dead yet.' And it was true, because the rainbow banner rippled as Peter breathed the smallest of breaths.

Then Curly did something very strange. He grabbed Hook's woolly cuff and said, 'Ask me. Ask what I want to be when I grow up.'

The ravelling man tried to pull away, but he could not.

'Don't, Curly!' begged Slightly. 'Do you want to be like me? All grown up, so that Peter hates you? All grown up so you can never fly home again?'

Curly gripped tighter. 'Ask me.'

Ravello winced. 'Very well. What does Curly want to be . . .'

'A doctor. I want to be a doctor!' In fact Curly wanted and wanted it so much that he grew, then and there. Peter Pan needed a doctor, so Curly wished, and soon enough there he stood, a grown doctor with a head full of cleverness and a pocketful of instruments. Sometimes grown-ups are the only people who can help.

With a broken swordfish sword and a pair of sugar tongs, Doctor Curly Darling drew from Peter's chest a strand of woolly grey. It was not poison from Hook's

little bottle. It was not blizzardy snow. It was not smoke
from the burning Neverwood.

It was a wisp of London fog.

Wendy had brought it to Neverland
caught in her handkerchief.

Peter took a long, shuddered breath and sat up.

His combed hair blew into tangles.

His bad temper blew away and he leapt to his feet.

'Now I shall fight you, Hook!' he cried, snatching up the broken sword. 'You can keep your treasure—I don't want it—but I'll take your life instead!' And so saying, he ran at the ravelling man.

The blade only snagged harmlessly in the shaggy wool. Ravello's hook flashed in the sun.

It grazed Peter's face.

It ripped Peter's shirt and hoiked him into the air.

'NO!' cried the children and hid their eyes.

So they did not see where Puppy came from.

Little Puppy. Just once he had sunk his teeth into Ravello, and in that moment the circus master had asked if he wanted ever to be a big dog. Ravello's magic had done its work. Now Puppy was back, and silly as before, but much, MUCH bigger.

He pounced on Hook—took another bite of the strange-tasting wool. His teeth snagged, his paws got tangled and although Puppy was the gentlest and silliest puppy in the world, he did what no one else could do . . .

'Are you dying, Mr Ravello?' asked Wendy afterwards.

'I fear so, Miss Wendy.'

'I will put your treasure here, where you can see it. You should sleep now. Sleep is a great healer.'

'Madam, I have not slept for twenty years. Not since the crocodile.'

'Maybe there's been no one to kiss you goodnight,' said Wendy.

'Not since the crocodile.'

'Madam, I *never* had anyone to kiss me goodnight,' said Ravello.

So Wendy laid the scarlet jacket over him and kissed him on the cheek. 'Goodnight, Mr Ravello.'

'Hook! My name is James Hook,' whispered the unravelled man, and closed his eyes.

Peter was furious. 'You kissed my enemy! That makes you my enemy too!'

And he cut a door in the air and banished Wendy to Nowhereland.

On the other side of the closed door, Wendy did not look very banished.

After a moment, she picked up an imaginary rock and threw it through the imaginary glass door—SMASH!

'Bosh and tosh, Peter,' she said, stepping back carefully through the broken glass. 'Sometimes you are such a ninny.'

Curly unrolled the map. (He could read now, of course. Doctors can.) 'Hook lied,' he said. 'It is not called the Maze of Witches at all. On here it is called "the Maze of Mothers".'

That's right. The women in the Maze were not witches wanting to *eat* Lost Boys. They were mothers come looking to *find* their Lost Boys and take them home again. But I'm sure you knew that all along. No mother could ever forget a lost child or stop looking until that child is found.

'Splendid!' said Wendy. 'We cannot fly home because we have no shadows. Anyway, Curly and Slightly are too grown up for magic. There is only one thing to do.'

So back they went to the Maze of Mothers—Slightly, Curly, the Twins, and Tootles—to find the mothers who had lost them when they were babies.

Trapped in the rocky labyrinth, the Mothers were still searching, of course, still weeping and hoping—always hoping—to find their lost ones.

'Mine won't be here,' said Slightly.

'Oh yes, she will,' said Wendy.

'Mine won't want me now I'm big,' said Curly.

'Oh yes, she will,' said Wendy.

'I'm going to stay here and marry Peter!' declared Tootles.

For the first time that anyone had seen, a look of pure fear came into Peter's eyes. Luckily Wendy came to the rescue. Quick as a wink, she gave Tootles a sharp push—'Oh no, you're not!'—and tumbled Tootles into the Maze.

'Thank you, Wendy,' said Peter.

'You're welcome,' said Wendy.

Slightly's mother was still holding his favourite toy.

Curly's mother had come looking for a boy, but was perfectly happy to find a full-grown doctor instead. (Doctors are almost as special as children.)

The Twins' mother told them their proper names. And do you know? They thought that 'Marmaduke' and 'Binky' were the best names in the world. The Maze of Mothers is a sorry place a-trickle with tears. But that day three mothers found perfect happiness, because they found their lost children.

Tootles's *father* found her. He knew his son at once, despite the ballet dress and plaits. 'About time too!' he growled. Then he threw his wig in the air and jumped for joy.

John and Wendy did not need a mother: he and Wendy had never been lost. But they did need a way of getting home. So John busied himself lashing together all the prams to make a raft. By the time he finished there was room for everyone—even Puppy.

For a moment, Wendy thought she could not bear to leave Peter all on his own in Neverland.

'Stay here, then, and play,' said Peter with a shrug. 'So long as it's not weddings.'

But Wendy-grown-up was a mother, and even Wendy-the-girl could remember a little girl called Jane waiting at home for her. So kissing Peter's cheek, Wendy leapt aboard, just as the raft moved out to sea.

'One day your own mother will come and find you!'
she called, but Peter quickly put his fingers in his ears.
He hated all talk of mothers.

Peter watched the raft sail away into a brightness of
sea. Then he turned his back and set off for the
Neverwood.   There were
adventures calling to him
and games that needed
playing . . .

Far away, on the slopes of Neverpeak, Ravello the ravelling man slept for the first time in twenty years. It is true what they say: a good sleep makes everything better.

When he woke, it was not Ravello but James Hook who slipped his arms into the scarlet jacket. It became him. He became it. Clothes can do that.

As for his hatred of Peter, well, even inside the crocodile, that had never unravelled. Now it was as good as new.

'Have at you, Peter Pan,' he whispered under his breath. 'Revenge will be sweet when you and I next meet.'

The Neverwood grew back green. Peter's shadow grew back too, in time. So now he can fly again, and come and go, just as he chooses.

Maybe one day he will fly in at your window and show you Hook's map of Neverland.

If you smile and say 'please', he may even take you there.

HOW THIS BOOK CAME ABOUT

First it was a play. Then it was a book. During the early years of the twentieth century, the story of Peter Pan was a runaway success which made James Matthew Barrie the most successful author in Britain.

In 1929, Barrie made a remarkable gift to his favourite charity. He gave away all his rights in Peter Pan to Great Ormond Street Hospital for Sick Children. This meant that whenever anyone staged a production of the play or bought a copy of *Peter Pan and Wendy*, the hospital would be richer for it, instead of Barrie. Over the years, it has proved a more valuable gift than he could ever have imagined.

In 2004, Great Ormond Street Hospital decided to sanction, for the very first time, a sequel to the book *Peter Pan and Wendy*. They held a competition to find, from among authors all over the world, someone to continue Peter's adventures in Neverland. Geraldine McCaughrean won that competition. *Peter Pan in Scarlet* is the book she wrote, and it became an international bestseller. Now you can read the same story in this illustrated edition, with a new version of the text, specially adapted by the author, and beautiful artwork from David Wyatt.